a

girl

and

her

gator

a girl and

by **sean bryan**

illustrations by **tom murphy**

her gator

ARCADE PUBLISHING / NEW YORK

This is the story
of a girl named Claire,
who discovered a gator
on top of her hair.

"Excuse me," she said,
"I usually share, but I'm not sure
I want you staying up there."

"Just let me hang out," said the gator, Pierre, "These views are amazing, and I love the fresh air!"

"But my friends will all
whisper and gossip and stare.

The gator just
smiled and said,

"Au contraire!

You can do anything
with a gator up there.

You could go to the fair with a gator up there.

Or give your brother a scare with a gator up there.

You could be a zillionaire with a gator up there!

Or even eat an éclair, as long as you share

snippity snappity

with that

gator up there."

"I see what you mean,
   we could be quite the pair!"
          said the girl named Claire
          to the gator, Pierre.

"But I do have a question. There's one little snare.

What should a girl wear with a gator up there?

Swimwear?

Skiwear?

Evening wear?

Pirate wear?"

You'll always look pretty,

you'll always have flair,

when you are the girl

with the gator

up there.

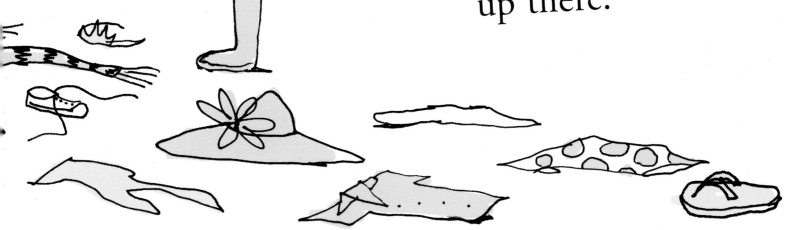

So off to ballet went

the gator and Claire.

And her friends **did** whisper, and people **did** stare.

"How cool is that? She has a gator up there!"

What could
be better?
What else
could compare?

She said,

"Have you met my cousin

who lives in Bel-Air?

He woke up attached to a Kodiak bear."

For Grace Drugge, a wonderful neighbor/niece — SB

For Julie, Ellis, and Van — TM

FIRST EDITION

Library of Congress Cataloging-in-Publication Data

Bryan, Sean.
  A girl and her gator / by Sean Bryan ; illustrations by Tom Murphy.
    p. cm.
  Summary: One day, a girl discovers an alligator on her head and, although she is afraid her friends will laugh, the 'gator soon convinces her that she can still give her brother a scare, eat an éclair, and choose anything to wear as long as he is there.
  ISBN-13: 978-1-55970-778-5 (alk. paper)
  ISBN-10: 1-55970-798-4 (alk. paper)
  [1. Alligators—Fiction. 2. Humorous stories. 3. Stories in rhyme.] I. Murphy, Tom, 1972– ill. II. Title.

PZ8.3.B829Gir 2006
[E]—dc22   2005029291

Published in the United States by Arcade Publishing, Inc., New York
Distributed by Hachette Book Group USA

Visit our Web site at www.arcadepub.com

10 9 8 7 6 5 4 3 2

Designed by Tom Murphy

Imago
Printed in Singapore